DEMPSEY AND MAKEPEACE

Season 1 – Episode 1

KAY J. WAGNER

ISBN 9781090737540

A mon fils, Vincent.

Season 1 - Episode 1 : « Armed and extremely dangeroux »

Summary : «*New York Police Lieutenant James Dempsey kills his corrupt partner Joey and has to lay low until the case can be further investigated. His superior O'Grady sends Dempsey to London, England as part of an exchange of officers. Chief Superintendent Spikings, head of SI10 is not to pleased to have a 'yank' forced onto his department. He decides to couple Dempsey with his complete opposite, Sergeant Makepeace, an upper class English rose on a case involving a mysterious shipment of caviar..... ».*

A fan pushes the warm air in the room, on the wall a photo up two men smiling at the goal. In the half-light, man reloads his gun, he introduced the balls one by one in the barrel and puts it on his desk while the phone rings.

— Dempsey, said. Yes, is what time Joey? Okay, sure, I'll be there.

A car drives on the docks, it's night, his headlights light low places. Dempsey stops, there a small cigar in his mouth, he looks at a man sitting in his truck, Joey. The man made a small nod of his head. The two men descend from their vehicle.

— Then Champion, ready for the big bang? It might be good

this time.

— I've heard this song somewhere, says Dempsey.

— Oh you know, confess.

— You can still feel the bender you took yesterday, said Dempsey.

— The case is in the bag, we'll be entitled to our photo tomorrow in the press!

— Oh, yes? Dempsey says smoking his cigar.

— Yes, but not like the first time...you remember? he said by the grimace of the photo that Dempsey has hung in his office where they wince both.

— So, you've made progress since then.

— Yes thank you, says Joey.

— Why have you begun suddenly alone? Usually, we work together.

— We are, all right? says Joey patting the cheek with one hand. Come on come on, quite discussed it.

Joey was in his pickup with Dempsey. They arrive at the docks where merchant ships are moored. Men fish along the quay while a man warms the hands near an open cask in which burns a fire. Dempsey and Joey come down from the truck, they approached the rear of the vehicle to pick up their fishing gear.

— You spotted him?

— No, not yet. I'd drop the bag in front of him.

— Okay, says Dempsey with his cane in fishing and the box hooks.

The two men come forward and made Joey falls his canvas bag near a group of two men. Dempsey bends down to pick it up, his gaze crosses that of a seated man.

— We set up here, said Joey by designating a place a little more away.

The two men sit on a small piece of concrete.

— He said it was hidden in a small brown bag, said Joey.

— Okay, Dempsey replied, securing it with his teeth, one of the small fishing line sinkers and turning his head to his left where he sees the man earlier, at his feet lies a small paper bag.

— Eddy heading type, they will exchange a few words, he will give her the bag and it falls on him.

— I wish that it happens before the fish starts to bite, said Dempsey glancing towards the Eddy.

— Colt may not have happened, says Joey.

— What? asked surprised Dempsey.

Joey takes a sip of alcohol contained in a vial glancing to his right while a Brown car comes slowly on the docks, a wheel a man.

— Joey, I don't like it at all! said Dempsey, when he saw the car near them.

— what? What don't you like? says Joey looking straight in front of him.

— Did anyone else! asked worried Dempsey.

— No, only in you, why?

— The boss just showed up!

— Coltrane ?

— Coltrane! You want to laugh!

— It smells not good Joey!

Eddy raises his cane fishing, takes his paper bag and rises. Heading the car and Dempsey looks at him from the corner of the eye. Then he gets up and Joey rises in turn.

— He headed to Coltrane, said Dempsey. He will give the bag to Coltrane!

— Then Coltrane is probably the guy who..says Joey.

But Eddy goes near the car, walk in the direction of Joey and Dempsey. Joey out his revolver from his belt and back together in the back of Dempsey, who turns around and grabs her arm.

— Get Eddy! yells Joey.

A gunshot is heard and Eddy fled. Coltrane left the scene at the wheel of his car while Dempsey sends Joey in the ground, turns around and pulls out his gun from his jacket. He shoots Joey who was trying to recover.

— You have not the Joey, he said still watching in shock. You wouldn't, he repeats off hearing a police car siren.

In the 9th district police station, Dempse has a heated discussion.

— You hear me o' Grady! Scream Dempsey while walking in the hallway. Coltrane is a bastard! Look, nothing can stop me to say what I think of this bastard!

— Come on, old man down!

— Coltrane! screaming Dempsey. It's low enough that!

— Come on Dempsey, you lose the head, said O'Grady by opening the glass door of his office. It will be of Coltrane's word against yours!

— Give me 48 hours! Not one of more to find him, the famous Eddy! And I'd spit out what he knows, even if I have to hang him by the thumbs!

— You would be able to identify it if you'd find? asked O'Grady.

— Ah sure !

— So take a glance on it, told him by launching a folder on his desk.

Dempsey opens the folder and discovered pictures of a dead man, Eddy.

— It was discovered when?

— Yesterday, late in the day, said O'Grady.

— After that I submitted my report, says Dempsey based photos.

He took a few steps in the office passing the hand through his thick brown hair. With both hands, he then balance Baskets placed on your furniture close to the pot of coffee and removes his jacket of rage.

— This can lead very far, is this not?

— Yes, well beyond Coltrane.

— Since we are here, I want to fix him now! replied Dempsey

heading to closed the office door.

— Stop it! Stop it! shouted O'Grady.

— So what? What did I have to lose! You're next on the list! he shouts in beating the chest of the hand. If I have to take my skin, I'll take him with me!

— You don't have not digested the betrayal of Joey huh?

— I would have preferred that it was he who to get down! says Dempsey.

— This time, you will listen to me Dempsey! We'll get him Coltrane! But this isn't yet the time and the hour had come, I need you! he said pointing his finger at him.

— And me, what would I do in the meantime? The tapestry? Or diving with a bullet in the skull and cement soles?

— We'll put you on leave, says O'Grady.

— What?

— If I keep you here, they will get you! A mutation in another sector it won't! Well you know. When corruption has reached this point, you're safe anywhere, even here. It also you know, he said as he sat behind his desk.

— O'Grady, you let me down, huh? You want me to leave the service, right? After all these years, I have not yet the right to retirement! To you - what do I do, I get a job elsewhere? he starts yelling.

O'Grady looks at him while Dempsey sits on a chair in front of him.

— I'm a cop, I've always done that, he said, shaking his head.

And I can't do anything else, he said looking O'Grady.

In the office of Bologna.

— We found you a small nice hideout in London, England.

— England ? repeat Dempsey.

— England, repeat the man sitting in a chair behind a desk.

— Five thousand kilometres of New York, the suburbs, said O'Grady.

— Vous connaissez l'Angleterre ?

— No !

— You'll enjoy, my wife and I, we went there two years ago, and we are more.

— What kind of safe house? request Dempsey.

— An exchange of staff with the British police, says O'Grady. It is a common practice, we send them here and they send us there. Bologna arranged to keep you lot.

— You will be attached to a new team they had, everything there is discreet, almost illegal.

— Nothing in the file, or on computer, said O'Grady.

— The British without very much unlike us, said Bologna.

— You will make the same kind of job you did here.

— Except that no one will know who you are, said Bologna.

— And that nobody here will be aware, said O'Grady.

— Except for you two, said Dempsey.

— Nobody, says Bologna.

A car drives in the direction of Kennedy Airport, O'Grady of driving and at his side on the passenger seat is Dempsey. The car stops in front of one door of access while raindrops crashing on windows.

— We find sandwiches with salami in London? asked Dempsey.

— It will send by mail, said O'Grady.

— Butter, with pickles.

— I'll see in person.

— What's in London, it's like Los Angeles, it moves in the car?

— You have kept your credit card? Rent a car on arrival, you will see well.

— It was escorted, Dempsey, watched the car parked behind them.

— Forget it, said O'Grady.

Dempsey opens the door and gets out of car.

— Suppose that a reception Committee waiting for me in London? he said.

— No one knows that you go.

— If that happened, I warn you, I their Squire their account, and I would stay set yours and that of Bologna!

— And Coltrane ?

— Your first, says Dempsey by not leaving your eyes.

— You say that I saved you from death Dempsey! says O'Grady.

— Maybe it's me O'Grady who saved yours! Dempsey replied, grabbing his backpack.

He slammed the door without greenhouse hand O'Grady tends him. Bologna gets out of his car and joined O'Grady.

— Do you think that the British will be able to train it? said O'Grady, looking at Bologna.

— They have well trained Argentines!

— Yes, it's still a chance that he's a regular. Imagine for a moment that Dempsey is involved?

Dempsey will stop a few moments in front of the entry door, he his returns and look straight ahead it this city that he is about to leave. Then it passes the access doors.

In a London building, Spikings Superintendent and with the Sergeant Chase.

— It took us ten thousand hours of work to prepare this case! he said by launching the desktop.

— Well, I'm afraid that the advocate general decides in view of the current political climate, the record discloses more than 60% chance of success before the proceedings. I'm sorry Mr. Superintendent, he said rising from his chair.

Spikings do a nod to Chase to follow.

— Ah, Spikings, bad news from C division, they have available, I mean who is the height, said an official in uniform.

— If there was less money in their gadgets as their riot shields, maybe we could have …

— Don't get too excited, maybe I'll see what need you, someone very competent.

— What Department? request Spikings while out at the foot of the building load.

— It is not to tell the truth from us, it is part of the experimental Exchange with the New York Police.

Spikings stops suddenly and Chase who walks behind him arms cluttered with binders, lack of hit him.

— You give me one of those Yankee cursed! request Spikings.

A from New York TWA plane lands on Heathrow Airport near London. Dempsey presents itself at the car rental counter.

— Hello, I need a car, he said to the hostess. Of course, if I needed a sandwich, I would go elsewhere. Do not pay attention to what I say, it's Jet lag, he said.Il sort son portefeuille et prend une carte de crédit.

— You take these cards? he asked.

— But of course Sir, she told him.

— Perfect. There was a limit probably?

— No, would what car you?

— Well, it's for an old friend, he called O'Grady and I would like to surprise her, so I would like your the most expensive model! he said.

Spikings inspector enters offices at no charge. The men are

civilians ringtones phones sound, it is followed by Chase.

— Something tells me, Chase, that day will still be charged! he said, sitting on his chair.

— Yes, he's here, said Chase by picking up the phone. The boss, said looking Spikings.

— What is it?

— Another murder in Springfield Market, says Chase.

At the airport, Dempsey is about to recover his rental car a driver station two of him, it's a white Mercedes-Benz convertible.

— So, if I understand it, I don't have to follow the boulevard to the place indicated, that is it? He asked the hostess accompanying the vehicle.

— This is here, she said to him by giving him the brochure.

The driver out of the vehicle on the right side.

—And thanks for the tip for the apartment, I'll be visiting, but it's as if it was done, he said dropping his hand luggage on the back seat of the convertible. He opens the door left side of the vehicle, sits down and is about to put his hands on the steering wheel.. .which is visibly absent.

His reaction laughed the hostess.

Warehouse Price Bros, Spikings and Chase went to the scene of the murder, they cross the aisles where are hanging carcasses of beef. Doors improvised with blue plastic were developed to preserve the crime scene. They are both in a huge fridge where a police officer take pictures. The body of a man dressed in a blue blouse is lying on the ground on his stomach.

— When did it happen? request Spikings.

— About three o'clock in the morning. A cold room, it's rather curious, says Chase.

— Is there any witnesses?

— I brought the flying squad immediately, they have questioned two or three.

Spikings leans close to the man and look at the contents of one of his hands open.

— What is it? he asks pointing to a small gray grains.

— Caviar, there many pockets, says Chase.

Dempsey through London, he meets the changing of the guard outside Buckingham Palace. At the Springfield Market, a police truck parked nearby, a man with a moustache is approaching and look agitation.

In his office, Spikings does a drawing when Chase enters his office.

— Someone for you, a weird guy Sam Johnson.

— As he enters, he said while continuing to draw.

Dempsey comes into the office.

— Well well, what do you have interesting? request Spikings without raising the head.

— Dempsey. Dempsey of the New York City Police Lieutenant, said asking his badge on the desk of Spikings. Now in the report, he said sitting on a chair.

— Who gave you this car in which you came?

— I rented it at the airport.

— You're going to keep it long?

— Until O'Grady refuses to pay the note.

— And it can depend on what?

— This depends on the degree of guilt he feels towards me.

— Keep in mind that I don't would provide you never the opportunity, says Spikings.

— Hopefully, Dempsey replied looking him in the eyes.

— And that I accept threats from anyone! replied a firm tone Spikings.

— More than me, said Dempsey a smile to the lips.

— And above all, of a Yankee!

The Tragg International Truck leaves the warehouse. Dempsey and Spikings arrive by walking to the warehouse.

— Six months ago, another handler was killed, said Spikings. We believed in an accident and then rumors came to the ears on a truckload of caviar.

— Charge of caviar? repeat Dempsey.

— Caviar! The weird is that he was not insured, in any case, person has never claimed.

— You asked all companies?

— London Yes, if he had been insured abroad, the Lloyds would have been aware.

— Idea of the market value of a truck of caviar?

— More than my annual salary. replied Dempsey.

— A 40-ton trailer, it must be in the 16 million pounds sterling.

— And in dollars ?

— Once and a half.

— I see, he said, whistling. And, the truck never arrived?

— Not to our knowledge. He perhaps never existed.

— Tons of caviar, it must require thousands of bottles of champagne to digest! What is known where they came from?

— Excellent question! I guess it comes from a stock looted in Iran after the revolution.

— And the victim, he was probably aware of certain things?

— Not until yesterday in all cases either, I would know.

— What do you mean ?

— Yesterday, he had made contact with me, it was one of my men, and even one of the best.

He takes out a cigarette and Dempsey out his lighter and it gives of the fire.

— Sorry, I know how it feels, said Dempsey.

— What is important is when they tortured him, if they had discovered who he was.

— In New York, the mobsters kill a cop that last spring, said Dempsey.

— Here it's the same, but I don't want to take any chances. I have another detective that he too is on this case, Sergeant

Makepeace. It's going to take more, but this time in broad daylight.

— It is preferable.

— I have an idea, if you were together. I mean, since the chance put you on the case... Yes? Sergeant Makepeace could make you aware of our methods.

— Suppose that we hear not?

— Come on, I believe you will hear you, replied Spikings.

Ils entrent tous deux dans un bar.

A waitress wearing a black mesh pantyhose is at the bar, waiting for his order. She put down her tray on a table and a man sitting all around him is a slap on the buttocks. She turns around and slap him a slap on the face.

— No, but! That I stay you there, rude man, she said.

It clear the table of empty glasses and returns to the bar.

— Sharon, be friendly with customers please! the manager told him.

— It's good, it's going, they love that we send them a walk, you know! he answers it.

— Look, you have a huge hole in your tights! he said.

— And you, it might make you a huge hole in the head if you get me the way! he said pushing it with his tray.

A man comes back and takes her in his arms, he's the man with the mustache of the warehouse.

— Ah, I guess......, he said with a smile.

— That's enough Phil, she said pushing him gently.

— I go out clubbing tonight, come with me? he asks her.

— No thanks.

— Here, he said by sliding a ticket in her bustier.

— That's nice, but it commits to nothing, she told him.

—57 in port place West End. You'll like it.

— Yes, but I have a husband, you forget.

— Bring him, tell her it's me who invites him.

She's going back to the room with her tray of drinks.

Spikings and Dempsey enter the room.

— If one of your men is here, let me guess, said Dempsey. He's a c.i.?

— Not really.

They can be installed both at a table and the waitress put his tray down on their table.

— It be for you? she asks them.

— A blonde, he says Spikings.

— Scotch on the rox, said Dempsey.

— I'm sorry Sir, but you have a rox, will settle for crushed ice, said rid the table of empty glasses.

— Look, I'm looking for a man named Harry Mak, you know who it is? He said Spikings while she left their table.

— Assuming that Yes.

— Tell tell him I want to see him urgently, on the part of his head, Spikings by looking at.

— You're a cop, cops I can sniff them 100 meters!

— When you see him, tell him that expected this afternoon in the warehouse.

— If I have not forgotten! she told him.

Dempsey slipped a ticket on its tray.

— Here, for you my lovely memory, he said.

Dempsey looks around.

— After a brief overview, I concluded that your man is not here, he said.

— You just talk to him, Spikings says.

Dempsey look Spikings making him sign that 'yes' head. He turns abruptly, and look at the waitress.

In his room, the waitress removes her dress and then her pantyhose in Black mesh, tie her bra, takes his gun and slipped into his Holster over her blouse. She readjusts his as well as his bow tie black leather jacket, check her outfit.

In the office of Spikings, Dempsey fell asleep on a Chair, the file on his knees which pictures are dropped on the floor.

— I want that this Embassy is protected 24 hours a day. About, the perks that you do to sell your awful bouquets me are immediately communicated, understood?

The young woman enters the office of Spikings, she removed his jacket and goes before him.

— Sergeant, said Lieutenant Dempsey of the New York Police, glancing at the sleeping man. Lieutenant, Lieutenant!

Dempsey is the head and looks.

— Sgt. Makepeace said Spikings, presenting the young woman.

It is a very beautiful young woman with short blond hair wearing a Cup to the square plunge on sides, beautiful blue eyes and a perfect silhouette.

— Nice to meet you, said Dempsey.

— Me, she said stepping up to him and shook his hand.

— You are aware for Willis?

— Yes to the bar, everyone talked about him she responds.

— You have learned something?

— It left me time! she told him.

— No, you risked being burned!

— And how?

— He was tortured, said Dempsey while using a cup of coffee.

— I was forced to remember, said Spikings.

— You haven't finished treating me like a kid! She said. Whenever I come across a big deal…..

— Sergeant! Spikings interrupts him. Lt. Dempsey is in internship with us for some time. He is somewhat aware of the purpose of this investigation, I want you there worked together. Show him how we operate, and we may be able to take advantage of its own methods. His superiors in New York say the greater good, and who knows, you can team!

They look both determined to get gauge.

Dempsey see different pictures of the record.

— Price, that's the name of the firm worked Willis. No one knew it was the police, she said. Two brothers, Dan and Tom Price. Here is Dan, she said pointing to a photo of the man, at the exit of the Nugget Club where you were this afternoon.

— This one, who's that? ask him by showing him the photo of the man with the mustache.

— Phil Parris, a regular at the club who never talks about what he does outside.

— It is the band?

—There seem to know a lot of things. There is an I don't know what I struggle to locate him. You'd swear to see, that he has already dealt with justice. He was at the club today before your arrival. Curiously, said sitting down behind his desk, he invited me to a party tonight, a little incongruous way.

— Where is ?

— At Grovenor Square.

— You should go there, said Dempsey.

— Impossible.

— Why ?

— I told him that I was married.

— He chose to give up?

— On the contrary, he told me to bring my husband!

— That's a smart guy, said Dempsey, smiling. This is what he's already seen your husband?

— No.

— For a night, I could pass for it? Is that what you say,

Sergeant?

— But, we are barely Lieutenant, he knows she responds.

— Well, you take the opportunity to meet, he said smiling. Give me your address, I'll pick you around 8.

Dempsey's parking in front of the House of Makepeace. It is a three-storey house combined. Three strikes of the Bell. Makepeace is installed at his office and tape in the machine. She wears a black dress fitted, gathered at the bottom of the skirt and the shoulders are bare, his hair is up, it is beautiful and elegant. She headed for the front door.

— Hey! say Dempsey and discover the young woman.

He enters the House arms encumbered with a huge bouquet of roses. He's wearing a tuxedo, black pants and white jacket. He follows her in the living room.

— But it's too much, it did not, she said looking red roses.

— But no, I beg you. You want them? he said holding out the bouquet.

It detaches a rose that it hangs in the buttonhole of his white jacket.

— But what Sergeant class! What chic! he said looking at her dress enhanced with a golden belt. Although the glasses?

She removes her glasses to work and put them on his desk.

— Well, are we ready? So on the way, we'll take my car, she told him.

— One moment, he said the young woman.

— Why ?

— We repeat our role, she said pointing to the slips on his desk. These are some ideas that I put on paper for you and for me.

He takes the slip and roll into a ball in his hands.

— Useless! he said in launching the ball of paper behind him.

— How?

— I know him by Choir: Sam Johnson!

— Sam who ?

—Your husband! Sam the macho! You didn't know you had married a hard, huh? I'll add something. Your friend Phil saw you your profession as a waitress a little olé olé Nugget Club, then in this dress and look distinguished, I'm afraid it's hard to believe that being together... he said.

— Listen to inspector, she said.

— Lieutenant.

— Anyway, me too I'm afraid that it does not go.

— And why ?

— How properly to play our role, if we have any chemistry! she said.

— I don't think this is necessary, there are couples who hate each other, we can do part! Isn't it Sharon?

Dempsey's parking in front of the 57 port Square. They come down both car and walks up to the house. The Interior of the House stands a pool overlooking an open garden. Servers sneak between the guests their tray by hand.

— Sharon! said a man coming towards them.

— Phil! she said seeing him.

— I hesitated to you recognize, he said. The husband that you talked to me? ask Phil glancing Dempsey.

— Yes. Sam, this is Phil Parris, a regular at the Nugget, it was he who invited us to the party, she said.

— Ah yes, said Sam Johnson of New York, enchanted, shaking the hand of Parris.

— An American? said Phil in looking Makepeace.

— Who like Europe and Europeans, add it by looking at the young woman.

— Happening there half of his time, she said.

— You just arrived? asked Parris.

— Yes, I come to matter, says Dempsey.

— For this only? asks Phil looking at the young woman.

— No, and also to see! said Dempsey passing his arm around the waist of Makepeace.

— And what are you Mr Johnson?

— I sell and I buy, I get companies and you?

— I do the same thing, him he responds with a smile.

— That's interested me!

A waiter comes near them and they each take a glass of champagne.

— What's your first name? asked Dempsey.

— Phil.

— This reception is in honor of who?

— Of a certain Moser.

— I'd like to meet her.

— He also I am sure, it is also in our branch. If you'll excuse me, I'll try to find it.

It stops behind Makepeace.

— That dress is beautifully, he said.

— Thank you, she said smiling.

Dempsey and Makepeace are walking by the pool.

— This dress you suits, said Dempsey. You're right, this guy is a little weird.

— Maybe it's us who him seem a little weird, she said.

Phil Parris joined the photographer of the evening and gives him instructions.

— Look at big Dany Price out there near the pillar, said Makepeace.

Dempsey looks at the man smoking a cigar in good discussion.

— Yes, it's him, he said.

— I wonder what he does here, is not the kind of world he frequents.

Parris joined a man upstairs while the photographer takes pictures of Dempsey and Makepeace.

— That does this mean? said Dempsey.

— My elegance will perhaps seduced him? she said.

— It is the one that was at the entrance! It did not interest earlier.

Dempsey look human which Parris was talking to a few moments earlier.

— I'm going to go powder my, I think it is better separate us a few moments, she said.

He looks at her to get away. Then, he put down his glass on a small table and produces a cigar from the inside pocket of his jacket. He sits and wears his cigar to his lips and released his lighter.

— Sam? said Parris arriving near him. Sam, this is the person I was telling you about.

— Yes, he said getting up.

— This is the person I told you about who buys and sells. Sam, Abel Moser.

— Lovely reception, said Dempsey shook his hand.

— Import and export ?

— Yes, in any sense, provided that it brings me! replied Dempsey.

— And can we know in which Department Mr Johnson?

— He just tell you all that to do, said Parris.

— Like you, I presume, said Dempsey in looking Moser.

— If you'll excuse me gentlemen, said Parris.

The two men sit.

— It me please that boy! said Dempsey.

— He has great quality, it is full of energy!

— Yes, I noticed indeed. But I am betting that your boyfriend is not happy to see me here!

— Ah yes?

— Yes, he wanted to take advantage of my absence to take my place with whom guess you ….

— No ?

— If! But, he makes illusions, I went back to my place and it'll work with champagne and caviar every night! Ah but like I think about it, you wouldn't be interested by a batch of caviar?

The man turns his head and looks at him at length.

The evening continues.

— Is it you please, is it you please, I want to make a toast! said Dempsey. My wonderful wife Sharon and we two!

The remaining guests raise their glasses to all.

— Oh that's beautiful, said a woman. This is a second honeymoon!

— They have even not spent a night together, said Moser, he has just landed!

— No, but don't worry, we're going to catch up! said Dempsey.

— You're drunk! he said Makepeace leaning toward him.

— You're wonderful, he said.

— Tell me Mr Johnson, said Moser, where do you get off when you come to London? The hotel or rent an apartment?

— Dear friend I'm sorry, but it's a secret! says Dempsey.

— Oh please! said a woman.

— It's a surprise. Baby, just relax, if you don't mind, I'll tell this if friendly assistance.

He leaves the table.

— I rented the suite honeymoon of Park Lane!

All assistance applauds. He will sit down again while Makepeace looks at him surprised and then all smiles.

— But any medal alas his backhand, he said. Sharon doesn't love me anymore! It's true, I swear. I stayed a long time advantage and after all this time, she didn't even... Sharon, I beg you, a little kiss?

She looks at him and opens eyes.

— Come on, a kiss, says a woman.

— Come on baby, said Dempsey.

He puts his hand on his cheek and kisses him passionately. She rejects him, to go and throw the contents of his glass of champagne in the face. He rises from his chair, takes his glass of champagne and throws the content in the face. She slaps him and leaves the reception.

— Sharon, Sharon, you're not going to do that, my Princess! he shouts.

Then he turns to the assistance.

— She worked as a waitress, but never bare breasts! he said.

Makepeace is flying while Dempsey is sitting in the passenger seat slightly sleepy.

— I'm sorry Lieutenant, but I will mention this in my report.

— What so? he said standing on his seat.

— That you were drunk.

— Ah you're wrong Sergeant! he said.

— Please! she told him.

— I had only two cups of champagne in the evening. But I know green plants which will have a hangover in the morning!

— I don't believe a word, she said.

— So cuff me! Take me to the station and pass me an alcoholtest! But I think it's better still trust me.

— Why ?

— Look in the mirror, and you will see a car behind us with two passengers. They're following us since that one is gone.

She take a look in the rear-view mirror while Dempsey him recite the plate number of the car behind them.

— Too bad that it took my car, with your could have call center and identify it.

— And now, what do we do?

— Well, we go to the Park Lane Hotel! he said.

— I want you to know …

— Look, when we do things, they must be all the way, or so we take the risk of getting burned permanently! told Dempsey. Got it?

— Understood, she said.

— Park Lane Hotel Management, he said. If they continue to follow us, we'll be fixed!

She parks in front of the hotel while a groom comes to open the passenger door. Dempsey drops and tends a travel bag. They

come both in the hotel. The Bellman opens the door of the suite.
They cross the living room and enter the room, Dempsey throws
his bow tie on the bed.

— You take the bed and me, the couch, she tells him.

Makepeace comes out of the bathroom, wearing a white robe
and holds a blanket in his hands. It crosses Dempsey who goes to
the entrance of the suite and that would put a pillow in the hands. It
retrieves the bag and is about to join the room.

— Good night Mr. Johnson, she said.

— If you are missing something, call me, he said.

— But of course Inspector! she said.

— Lieutenant! he said turning to her. Place-you-now! He
repeats. I have nothing against the rank of Inspector, I was, but I
want a lot, Lieutenant! he said with a big smile.

She looks at him and slips finally under his covers. Then, she
turned off the lamp light and looking for a position to sleep.

In the hallway, a groom carries on a platter a bottle of
champagne and two cups. He lays them on a small table, out the
magnetic card and a gun equipped with a silencer and into the suite
occupied by Dempsey and Makepeace. He enters the room and
sees two forms lying under the covers. He shoots with his revolver
on the forms. The bathroom door opens and Dempsey popped his
gun in his hand.

— Police! screaming Dempsey.

The two men exchanged gunfire. The pursuit continues in the hallway of the hotel. The man hustles a server that fall to the ground with his tray down the stairs.

— Stay down! shouted Dempsey.

The two men run down the stairs and arrive in the the breakfast room where clients are installed which sows panic. The man pulls in the direction of Dempsey, who lies on the ground. They cross the kitchen and exchanges of gunfire continues. But the man has more ammunition.

— That was your last ball! screaming Dempsey.

The two men fight with their bare hands. While the man shake his neck, Dempsey takes a flat on a shelf above him and strikes the man with. But the man grabs an axe to meat and Pounces on Dempsey who tries to push him away with all his strength. While he is about to hit him with the axe, a gunshot is heard and the man collapses on the ground, dead. Makepeace appears in the kitchen, his gun in his hand, she just take down the man.

— I wanted to have living, said Dempsey catching his breath. Thanks anyway, Sergeant! he said. What is that wake you up?

The next morning in the office of Spikings.

— A decoy, said Dempsey.

— A decoy? repeat annoyed Spikings.

— Yes, a decoy. The guy who gave the order to liquidate the Johnson believed that Johnson had learned some things that he and who work for him felt that they did not know. That's all!

— But the Johnson in question knew nothing! gets angry Spikings.

— I know, we're the Johnson! replied Dempsey.

— Me too, I know you are the Johnson! I'm paid to know!

— Well then, where is the problem? asked Dempsey.

— Let me ask you one last question. Whereas you were Johnson, you must certainly be well informed about the case and what the killers ….

— What the killers assumed that knew the Johnsons! say the two men in chorus.

— Yes, it even is! said Spikings.

— Tell him Sergeant! said Dempsey, looking at the young woman.

— Johnson claimed to know.. .the things about caviar, she said.

— Things, but what things? Spikings replied, raising their arms in exasperation.

— Some things, she said looking Dempsey.

— No one will know, we killed them! says Dempsey.

— Grrr! Gets Spikings shaking fists.

— Well Yes! They killed them without even waiting to know what Johnson knew exactly!

— They took them to have doubts! said Makepeace.

— That's what happened with Wilson! replied Dempsey.

— Willis! Except that he had found the truck! she told him.

— But Johnson knew absolutely nothing actually! says

Spikings.

— Yes, but they could have know! said Dempsey.

— You don't know anything! replied Spikings.

— Me ? he said.

— You and her! You two! exclaims Spikings.

— We knew nothing, isn't this Sergeant! exclaims Dempsey.

Spikings is sitting in his chair behind his desk.

— So, can I at least make a simple suggestion, without one moment mingle the way you want to conduct your business? says Spikings.

— Be clear! said Dempsey.

Spikings holds out his hand to sign stop.

— I will be! Instead of trying to pretend that you know what it is, why not... do not put you in hunting to find out where the caviar!

— You want my opinion? said Dempsey, snapping his fingers. It's a great idea! You could say that before!

— This is what I tried! replied Spikings of exhausted air.

— Very well! Sergeant? On the track! tell Dempsey glancing Makepeace.

Dempsey and Makepeace on city roads.

— At the Chamber of Commerce, it knows no Moser and company, nor Moser any, she said while she parking her mini in front of Harrod's stores. We just only to make door to door!

They make their way and join a stand.

— Hello, said Makepeace, approaching a man of a certain age.

— Miss Harriet! What a nice surprise! said the man rising to greet her.

— Hello Philipot! she said smiling into his hands. I introduce a friend, Mr Dempsey.

— Nice to meet you Sir, said him the man.

— And I Similarly! replied Dempsey all smiles.

— He is American! she said.

— Oh .., said Philipot.

— Philipot, I would like to send to Mr Winfield, caviar as a birthday gift. Half a book of Beluga on my account, you understand?

— It will be done my lady! he said leaving his notebook.

— I have a favor to ask of you.

— Which ?

— Some informations.

— About what ?

— About the.. .importateur of caviar, said lowering his voice.

— Is this person aware of your other activities? asks Philipot glancing Dempsey.

— Fear nothing Philipot, he knows what I'm doing.

Dempsey joined them with two cigars packaged by hand.

— Tell me, have you ever heard of a certain Moser? I admit that the opposite be surprised.

— Moser ?

— Abel Moser, adds Dempsey. You've seen some havanas? he says glancing Makepeace.

Makepeace takes two cigars and puts them in their place.

— Are Abel Moser, you sure of the name?

— Yes, says Dempsey.

— The caviar ?

— Exact! answer Dempsey and Makepeace.

— In this case, it must be the son of Maurice Moser.

— Maurice Moser? she repeats.

— Nicknamed Mr Caviar in the business, said Philipot.

— Oh yes! she said.

— I didn't know that son, we were dealing with Maurice before he died, he told them.

— And when was that? Dempsey asks him.

— At 50 years. And his brother took over, Graham Moser. And the company has changed its name.

— In one of? asks Makepeace.

— Star Trading Co, he said them.

Dempsey and Makepeace enter the offices of Star Trading Co. He closes the door and put his credit card he used to open the door.

— They are probably not there, told it by discovering the offices.

— What? she asks.

— Forty tons of caviar! he said.

— Start over here, I'll watch it here, she said pointing to the cabinets.

She begins to look at the countless documents placed on the desktop.

« Two hundred tons of olive oil for the Federal Republic of Germany, she read on a document.

Dempsey sits down on the chair behind a desk.

« Fifty tons of military surplus to the Bolivia», she read on another Bill.

— For generators no doubt, says Dempsey by opening one of the drawers of the desk.

— They sell everything! she said.

« 375 hindquarters of beef from Scotland of Price Brothers in Hamburg», she read.

Then, she takes the other document.

— Yet of the Price Brothers beef! she said in reading another Bill.

— Here you go, caviar! bed Dempsey. Check export. Fifty kilos of caviar traded against five thousand pairs of Jeans.

— Dated from when? she asks.

— April.

— Surely the goods offered to Philipot! she told him.

— Sold all at the Dortherster Hotel the entire batch, he read. Show me the beef! he said lifting the head.

She hands him the document and it compares the bills.

— This transport company with this kind of name « Tragg International », he said.

— Yes, I know, she said.

— And Price uses the same carrier as Moser, he said.

— So what ?

— So, that means that is perhaps not a coincidence?

It leans to the back of the chair and to tap the nose.

— This is it! exclaims standing on su file.

— What?

— The caviar is in beef!

She starts to laugh.

— Lieutenant! she told him.

— But think about it! Willis worked at the Price, and he had to put their hands in the caviar! In the truest sense of the word! And they executed him. And they deposited the body in another location. Nobody believed that Price could be suspect, because.. .because he was using them, he was its cover! The Price were in receipt of Moser, the Price, and named Phil Parris!

— With the respect that I owe you Lieutenant, there is a certain vagueness in your arguments! she told him.

— Believe me Sergeant, I nose, and my nose like the elephant never wrong!

— I have one too! she told him.

—And you don't feel anything? Finally, yet everything is consistent! Yesterday in the morning, Willis find caviar in the beef in the warehouse of his bosses! And it's still there, if it is more, it is that he has been moved by the Tragg!

— The Tragg International would be involved?

— And why not ?

— What do you propose Lieutenant?

— What I propose? Nothing at all! Let's just watch the prices and the next load of beef the Tragg move, we have to follow the trail wherever it goes!

— It's just you! she told him.

— But it can become an order, he said.

— An order to me? she responds him.

— Perfectly. I'm a Lieutenant, and you're not that Sergeant!

— Learn that here, there's no Lieutenant!

— Well, you have one now!

— I don't have any orders from him!

— Listen my pretty …

— I don't like that you play this with me!

— My apologies, he said.

— Still, I would add that it is a completely crazy idea!

— It doesn't matter, I wouldn't need you!

— Who said that I refused?

— Is that what you mean then?

— Que c'est stupide ….mais que j'accepte !

Dempsey and Makepeace are on a stakeout, they see a white transport truck that rolls on the road. It enters the warehouse, they sneak walk and amount to a Rams to watch in the night. Other trucks enter the warehouse. Dempsey observes the activity with its infra-red binoculars.

— Look at that? said Dempsey while men open the back of a truck.

— what? she asks. Let me watch!

She grabs the binoculars.

— They load the beef in a truck of one of those who just came in! he said.

— Not at all! It the dump and put it in the other two! she told him.

— Let me see it!

He returned to the binoclars.

— But what is that mean?

— I wonder, is that what you think? she said.

— I think they divided in two lots caviar.

— Well, you now have the evidence, that there are two tracks, she tells him.

— No, there is in my opinion a lot of caviar. It is the same track. If they distribute the goods, is to spread the risk, but it does absolutely nothing. Did I right or not?

— Du calme, vous avez raison, lui dit-elle.

— Thanks anyway, he said.

Two white trucks of the « Tragg International » roll on the road.

— That is what we will do, said Dempsey. You drive away in front of the trucks and you fall down in the middle of the road. I wouldn't be far willing to intervene.

Makepeace stop his mini cooper across the road, she gets out of the car while the two white trucks arrive, they stop while a police car and a classic car arrive against sense.

— Thank you for you be arrested, told the driver Makepeace.

The police car marks a downtime then continued on his way. Two men push Makepeace car on the side of the road and sends it in the bushes.

— No, don't do that! What is with you people? Here here's my card, I'm a police officer!

One of the two men did in him releasing a blow behind the head, and then he lifts her. While men return his car, another puts it in a black plastic bag and drop her in the bushes.

The police car crosses Dempsey at the wheel of his Mercedes-Benz convertible. Two cars stop.

— We got trouble gentlemen? He asks them. Hey take it easy! he said seeing them get to him. Gently! I'm a police officer!

The three men go out their weapons and Dempsey actually equally sheltering behind his car, and he managed to shoot the three fake police. While the radiator of his car lets out white smoke, he hears a white truck of without its trailer. He motioned for the driver to stop.

— Police! he says, pointing his card. I need your vehicle, he says catching the driver by the arm and forcing him to descend.

He boarded the truck, roll between cars and joined the main road. In the bushes, Makepeace moves and rolls on itself to meet up on the road. Dempsey moving at good speed and stops in time to see the form in the black plastic bag move on the road. He stops in disaster and runs toward the plastic bag he rips.

— Well, you have no idea! Strange place to go camping! Get out of there! he said.

Dempsey and Makepeace took off on board the truck cab.

— Here they are, caught up with it! says Dempsey when he saw the two white trucks ahead of them.

He approaches as much as possible.

— Well, you take the steering wheel, he said to Makepeace.

They exchange their seat in the cabin while Dempsey holds the steering wheel blocked beforehand the speed.

— Press the pedal, he said while he unlocks the speed. You're going to get as close as possible!

Dempsey moves out of the cabin, a foot on the footstool and hands gripping the outside mirror. Makepeace is approaching the truck in of doubling slightly.

— Closer! Closer! shouted Dempsey.

While she gets closer, he jumps on the scale of the truck. She let go the wheel a few seconds of fright! Then she sees him climb up the ladder and climb up on the roof of the trailer. It goes back to the height of the cabin where two men and jumped on the roof of the cabin.

— There's someone on the roof! shouts the driver. Give me your gun!

But Dempsey is faster and send punch in the face of the driver.

The passenger chooses to jump out of the truck and Dempsey is found clinging to the door, hands on the wheel of the truck. He takes out a fence that leads to a construction site and jumps on the side of the road while the truck spills and toggle in the construction site.

Makepeace stops and runs to Dempsey who is lying on the ground.

— Dempsey! Dempsey! she calls arriving near him while he's coming. Are you okay?

— Yes, fine, he said looking at her.

— Charlie 20 to the Central, I need help. I repeat, I need help! she says into his walkie-talkie.

But an explosion and Dempsey catches Makepeace in his arms to protect her. Explosions sound while the fire spreads to the truck and its trailer. They are both in the midst of a cloud of white smoke.

— What is that? said Makepeace while Dempsey picks up a piece of junk with electric wire.

— This isn't the caviar! he said.

Twenty men surround the site.

— Stay where you are! one of them shouts with a loudspeaker. Do not try to run away! You're under arrest!

They look both.

« Put your hands on your head, and move gently towards us! Suspicious move, we will draw! ».

They raise their hands and moving slowly toward the military.

A guard opened the cell where Dempsey, he is lying on the bed and gets up. He entered and removed his handcuffs. In the next cell, a guard releases Makepeace. Spikings comes forward to Dempsey and fixed in the eye, then Makepeace joined them. They leave all three places without a Word.

Dempsey turns and sees the man on reception in great discussion with the military.

—Shipping of these missiles was entirely legal, said breeder. She had the approval of the Ministry of defence and Foreign Affairs. The weapons had been purchased on behalf of a weapons dealer, whose reputation is more to do. The client for which they were intended, was also perfectly in rule! The accompanying documents had been overseen by the Attaché of the Embassy of the destination country.

They arrive at the car of Spikings, who opens the back door and gestured to Makepeace with a wave of the hand to go up there.

— The « Tragg International » is 150%, one of the most serious transport companies. She is in relationship with the Royal arsenals, and a few other manufacturer of weapons and ammunition.

He shut the back door suddenly.

— Moser is an Honourable intermediary that needs to be covered when the political situation in his clients is uncertain. But it is nevertheless supported by Western Governments. The five men killed, Lieutenant! Were special branch known as action and which depends on the MI5 service responsible for the close monitoring of the movement of weapons within the country.

They are all three at the charge in the offices of Spikings.

— If the merchandise was healthy, why hide it in the beef? asked Dempsey.

— To protect against the subversive agents that you were suspected to be! Spikings says. The devil take you! Do you need kill five men! You could have just one kill an and others only!

— Is that what is suspended you Mr or what? asks Makepeace.

—Of course you're suspended him! And not just you, it's all the service which will be suspended! Special Branch must scream vengeance and MI5 will claim our heads! And who could drop the axe in your opinion! said nervously lighting a cigarette.

— Something tells me, that might be it on me, said Dempsey from the doorway.

—That's your lot will be the least enviable Lieutenant, given the problems there, awaiting you in New York! Spikings is said to him. The Minister of Foreign Affairs will ask at your service your immediate recall in the United States!

Makepeace look at Dempsey looking in turn. Dempsey left the office.

Makepeace pushes the door of a pub, she enters and sees Dempsey sitting at the counter in front of a beer.

— What is the problems that await you in New York? Well? she asks.

— Nothing, he says shaking his head.

— Oh come on! she said. We're in it together!

— Some internal difficulties, but don't worry, it'll get better, he said.

— You have put out there also in trouble?

— Yes, it happens more often that my turn, he laughed a nervous laugh. Some say it's a vice, and others, that's part of my charm.

He put down his glass and left the counter. Makepeace looks at a softened air, then recovers.

— I wonder why I have not refused flatly to follow your intuition blasted! she said.

— My intuition was founded! he gets.

— It was a stupidity!

— I discovered the missiles.

— They had nothing to do!

— There is a relationship.

— Just a coincidence!

— No, I tell you that everything is connected.

— Explain yourself.

He looks at it and to tap the nose.

— Don't do again me not the shot of flair, that's enough! I'm sick of your hunches!

He grabs him by the arm and the strength to be sit.

— For me, it's a certainty! And that's because I made them fear that one redirects me to New York! And you, if you put your nose in their caviar, I bet you anything that you pay dearly!

He took a stool and sits in front of her.

—Why do you think that Willis had a hole in the skin? For a bit of caviar? And the kind you killed at the hotel, and that strange thing, the Special Branch or MI5 did claim the corpse! What is? And one at the prison that I spotted on the evening of Moser and who was chatting with your boss!

— And then what ?

— If the shipment of the missiles was legal, why go to so much trouble to kill so many people! Me, I'll tell you! Because we are both about to raise a very big deal! And, I see no other explanation! It smells bad, very bad! And for the moment, it is in the caviar!

He takes a breath.

— I did what I could, but you're also in the shot. I'm out of ideas. You are in your country, then you can play!

Makepeace arrives at the wheel of a mini cooper black and parks in the driveway of a White House. She approaches the glass door and knocks gently. A servant sees him and just him open.

— Hello, Abbott, she told him all smiles.

— Hello, Miss Harriet, I warn Lord Winfield, you've arrived, he said.

A man of a certain age dressed in a black tracksuit, biked to apartment outside on the terrace.

— Miss Harriet Sir, announces the servant.

— Hello dad, she said while moving towards the man.

— Hello my dear, said took in his arms and kissing affectionately.

The servant brings them a cup of tea.

— Dad, we agreed remember that you wouldn't ask me questions about my activities, and that I would do the same about yours, she said. Well, I just ask you today, even though it is contrary to our conventions, to give me a helping hand.

— What do you need?

— Informations.

— You specify ?

—My partner and I have learned that a Department of secret services have recently arrested two alleged Israeli agents suspected of attempted sabotage against a shipment of weapons destined for a country of the Middle East.

— This is not impossible, but what do you want to know?

— Only if this alleged Department exists.

— I'll probably disappoint you, the Department in question exists, he said. And two Israelis suspected of spying have been taken alive.

— We knew that, she tells him everything preparing a drink in the lounge.

— Well, to tell you the truth, I figured. But there is a detail that could put some balm to the heart. The Department in question, you see, has an official status and authority...

— I beg you dad, comes in, she said patting her shoulder.

— Oh this isn't a State secret since he retires shortly. My dear, it is that this Department has to Director, against Admiral Dufield! he said.

— The uncle Dufield? she said straightening himself from the couch. It is a little weird.

— And even altogether, he said. But we were not going to abandon it after all what he has done. This Department, whose mission is to material loading occasional inspections which are not our responsibility of course that we are aware of his movements by the manufacturers themselves was created so to speak! This isn't a Department, there is only this good old Dufield and a young intern who filled his pen and licking stamps. Oh, I forgot to thank you for the eggs of sturgeon.

— Ah yes, caviar, you have received?

—Yes, we delivered me this morning, I'm grateful. But, it's almost a waste of money, I got very much these months who had been sent to me by Dufield. He had found I don't know where one end of stock cheaply!

— Thank you, Dad, you're a love! she told him.

The Tragg International trucks arrive at a warehouse. Dempsey and Makepeace are on a stakeout in their car.

— If you want to go, there is still time! Dempsey told him.

— Don't tell nonsense, she said.

Dempsey gets out of the car while it restarts. Makepeace arrived in front of a huge building, while Dempsey sneaks at two steps from the entrance of the warehouse. Makepeace knocks at the door.

— Uncle Dufield? she said.

The man opens the door.

— Oh my god! he said on seeing. But, what a surprise! Come on in!

— As I was passing by, the idea came to me to bring you this, she tells him in her putting game.

— Oh you are the most adorable niece, Harriet, told her by kissing her. You're the living portrait of your mother, you know, he said looking at her. But where's Mark? Mark? We are completely overwhelmed at the moment, but I can tell you, it's a secret! I'll explain later, follow me, will you?

Meanwhile, Dempsey went into the warehouse. In the middle of the crates is a room surrounded by a thick wall of transparent plastic, inside computers work to full plans. Missiles are being programming.

Mark enters the room where Dufield and Makepeace, is the man who was at the party of Moser and Dempsey saw military prison.

— Mark my dear friend, you see, one of the advantages of old age is that you have visit your nieces who come to see you as Harriet!

— Yes indeed. Enchanted, he said the man shook his hand.

The man then leaves the room.

— Uncle Dufield, you feel well? ask Harriet.

— Yes Darling, but the day has been hard enough and if you have no objection, I'll go to bed, he said.

— Of course my uncle, she told him. Good night.

Mark's on the phone.

— Station 559 request special assistance, he said. Immediately.

In the warehouse, the programmer leaves the room and Dempsey took the opportunity to approach the missile.

Mark enters a work room where Phil Parris.

— Parris! Here, they are both. Search the shed, he said.

Dempsey is the piece of the missiles and inspect unions, comes out a box blue of caviar. He hears a noise and hides among funds. Parris entered the warehouse his gun in his hand. Dempsey let him move forward and then Pounces on him. The two men are fighting violently in the warehouse and Dempsey eventually knock him out with his fist.

Makepeace slowly enters the warehouse. Mark is behind it and applies his gun on his head. Dempsey out of the warehouse of his gun in his hand.

— Drop the gun or I'll shoot! shouted a man with a loudspeaker from a helicopter that illuminates the warehouse. I repeat, drop the gun!

Dempsey tries to spot the man in the helicopter.

— Obey! shouting Mark by holding one arm Makepeace.

Dempsey throws his revolver and arms up. Mark pushes Makepeace to Dempsey who made him sign that she couldn't do anything.

In a disused building, a man checks the explosives fixed on the Interior pillars, Parris. Using an iron bar, he opened a wooden box and backwards, Dempsey roll on the ground, hands and ankles tied and a sparadra on the mouth. Then, he opens the second fund where Makepeace.

Outside, a helicopter arrives and Lands on the roof of the building. Mark down and runs towards the Interior of the building. Parris raises Dempsey under the arm and drags up a pillar, he proceeds with Makepeace.

Dempsey and Makepeace look both.

— Check the explosives, said Mark Parris.

Then he approaches of Dempsey and Makepeace. He presses the switch before the launch of the process of explosion.

— I'll leave you ten minutes, this will give you time to confidences, if the heart tells you! he said to them.

He withdraws the tape over the mouth.

— Goodbye Lieutenant! Goodbay Sergeant!

The two men return to the floor.

— Well, we found our caviar, said Dempsey.

— Well Yes, she said.

— I'm sorry, he said looking at her.

— Too, she responds by looking up to him.

Outside, the two men are on the roof and are approaching the helicopter.

— How much time? request Parris.

— Ten minutes! replied Mark.

— I'm going to finish the job! he says pointing his revolver.

— Let's take off in five minutes! shouting Mark.

Mark runs to the helicopter and moved to the rear of the unit while Parris back to the room where are Dempsey and Makepeace. He down steps and headed them his gun in his hand.

He approaches Dempsey that he differs from his foot, then he looks Makepeace and directs his revolver to her. Dempsey took the opportunity to throw his feet attached to the arm and to drop his gun. Makepeace does the same and launches his two feet in the stomach of Parris.

— His gun! His gun! yells Dempsey.

In the helicopter, Mark checks his watch, there's 6 minutes before the explosion. In the building, Dempsey and Makepeace are back to back, she tries to drag him the gun in hands. He grabs the gun.

Outside, the helicopter starts to rise, but remains on site. Mark launches the stairs. In the warehouse, Dempsey and Makepeace are ready. She pull the trigger and the bullet releases their strings with the hands.

Opens the door to the roof and Mark see out Dempsey and Makepeace.

— Go ahead! Fast! screams Mark driver.

Dempsey puts his gun in the waistband of his jeans and short in the direction of the helicopter. While this amounts more, he catches just the rope ladder Il .

— Throw him out! Take altitude! screams Mark driver.

Parris came to its senses and popped up on the roof. He grabs the arm Makepeace and tries to hurl it into the void, while Dempsey goes up the rungs of the ladder. While she finds herself on the ground, she managed to flip Parris falling in a vacuum at the top of the roof of the building.

It is only a minute before the explosion.

— Let go Jack! screaming Mark by trying to bring down Dempsey.

But he comes out his revolver and him waved under the nose, then knocks him out a revolver.

— If you want to your skin, immediately come down or I'll kill you! yells Dempsey at the pilot.

The helicopter made a semi-circle and returns to the building. There are only 20 seconds before the explosion.

— Fast! Fast! screaming Dempsey to Makepeace coming running to the helicopter which is one metre above the roof of the building.

He grabs him by the arm and the helicopter takes off while Makepace has the rest of the body in a vacuum, but Dempsey hoist it up on board and keeps it on the floor of the helicopter.

The explosions in the building resonate and undermines somewhat the helicopter while the building is destroyed.

Spikings office door opens abruptly and Mark is projected on the desktop. The Superintendent rises precipitously his hand on his gun.

— That's the caviar! said Makepeace by launching the box caviar desktop Spikings.

— And that's the mole! said Dempsey.

— Alias Mark Savory, Deputy of Rear Admiral Dufield! she said. Who not content to inspect the missiles coming out of the country, meant that they are trapped! For potential opponents is able to detect the exact nature of the warheads which they were equipped.

— These information were worth a fortune! said Dempsey.

— But, the only way to pay for these services …

— Were to pay in caviar! said Dempsey.

They look both and Dempsey motioned him to go.

— You can guess the rest! said Dempsey glancing Spikings and out of the office.

— Dempsey ! said Spikings.

He takes the box of caviar, look at it and throw it to him. Then, he makes them the nod to go. Dempsey and Makepeace him smile and leave the premises.

— Ah I don't know how long more I did close the eye me! said Dempsey while they walk both near the Albert Hall. I'm going to bed early, I will try to find a hotel not too far for tonight, and I'd take tomorrow to find an apartment. Ah, but I think, the sequel to groom of the Park Lane Hotel is maybe free? he said.

— By the way, she said. I would like you to explain to me.

— What ?

He hands him the bottle of champagne and takes the box of caviar and eats a small spoonful of caviar.

— How is it that you have kept him and the idea came you for the occasion? she said.

— Ah, but it's the truth, but for another circumstance, to follow the advice of my father! he said.

— Ah yes ?

— Yes, he said, in a city where you don't know anyone, always book the suite for groom!

— Even if you are traveling alone?

— My father said again, an opportunity may still arise!

He hands her a spoonful of caviar.

END

Printed in Great Britain
by Amazon